Murder at Rutherford House

by Tom Chiodo and Peter DePietro

A Samuel French Acting Edition

SAMUEL FRENCH
FOUNDED 1830

New York Hollywood London Toronto
SAMUELFRENCH.COM

Copyright © 1990 by Tom Chiodo and Peter DePietro

ALL RIGHTS RESERVED

CAUTION: Professionals and amateurs are hereby warned that *MURDER AT RUTHERFORD HOUSE* is subject to a Licensing Fee. It is fully protected under the copyright laws of the United States of America, the British Commonwealth, including Canada, and all other countries of the Copyright Union. All rights, including professional, amateur, motion picture, recitation, lecturing, public reading, radio broadcasting, television and the rights of translation into foreign languages are strictly reserved. In its present form the play is dedicated to the reading public only.

The amateur live stage performance rights to *MURDER AT RUTHERFORD HOUSE* are controlled exclusively by Samuel French, Inc., and licensing arrangements and performance licenses must be secured well in advance of presentation. PLEASE NOTE that amateur Licensing Fees are set upon application in accordance with your producing circumstances. When applying for a licensing quotation and a performance license please give us the number of performances intended, dates of production, your seating capacity and admission fee. Licensing Fees are payable one week before the opening performance of the play to Samuel French, Inc., at 45 W. 25th Street, New York, NY 10010.

Licensing Fee of the required amount must be paid whether the play is presented for charity or gain and whether or not admission is charged.

Stock licensing fees quoted upon application to Samuel French, Inc.

For all other rights than those stipulated above, apply to: Samuel French, Inc.

Particular emphasis is laid on the question of amateur or professional readings, permission and terms for which must be secured in writing from Samuel French, Inc.

Copying from this book in whole or in part is strictly forbidden by law, and the right of performance is not transferable.

Whenever the play is produced the following notice must appear on all programs, printing and advertising for the play: "Produced by special arrangement with Samuel French, Inc."

Due authorship credit must be given on all programs, printing and advertising for the play.

ISBN 978-0-573-69195-9   Printed in U.S.A.   #15221

IMPORTANT BILLING AND CREDIT REQUIREMENTS

All producers of MURDER AT RUTHERFORD HOUSE *must* give credit to the Authors of the Play in all programs distributed in connection with performances of the Play and in all instances in which the title of the Play appears for purposes of advertising, publicizing or otherwise exploiting the Play and/or a production. The names of the Authors *must* also appear on a separate line, on which no other name appears, immediately following the title, and *must* appear in size of type not less than fifty percent the size of the title type.

No one shall commit or authorize any act or omission by which the copyright of, or the right to copyright, this play may be impaired.

No one shall make any changes in this play for the purpose of production.

Publication of this play does not imply availability for performance. Both amateurs and professionals considering a production are *strongly* advised in their own interests to apply to Samuel French, Inc., for written permission before starting rehearsals, advertising, or booking a theatre.

No part of this book may be reproduced, stored in a retrieval system, or transmitted in any form, by any means, now known or yet to be invented, including mechanical, electronic, photocopying, recording, videotaping, or otherwise, without the prior written permission of the publisher.

Murder at Rutherford House was first performed September 10, 1986 Off-Broadway in New York City at the original Rutherford House Mansion on Second Avenue and Fourteenth Street. Written and directed by Tom Chiodo and Peter DePietro, it was produced under the auspices of their theatre company, Murder A La Carte with the following cast (in order of appearance) and crew:

QUENTIN HOTCHKISS .... Quentin Crisp
MILLICENT, LADY RUTHERFORD
.... Patricia Michael
CAMERON WORTHLESTON .... Mark Ritter
SARAH RUTHERFORD .... Andrea Davis
HERMIONE RUTHERFORD .... Irma St. Paule
WENDLE WEEDLE, PI .... William Simington
OSWALD, LORD RUTHERFORD ....
.... Lee H. Doyle
BARONESS GRETA VON KEEPSEMFRUMFLOPPEN
.... Sharon McNight
CAMILLE RUTHERFORD .... Beth Broderick
CHADWICK STERLING .... Carleton Carpenter

Musical Director .... James Followell
Stage Manager .... Tony Hamill
Company Manager .... Louis Chiodo

In October 1987 *Murder at Rutherford House* began its first international tour in Singapore. The tour was directed by Tom Chiodo and Peter DePietro with the following cast (in order of appearance):

RUBY PINKBOTTOM*..............................Casey Wayne
MILLICENT, LADY RUTHERFORD...........................
.... Susan Tabor
CAMERON WORTHLESTON .... Mark Ritter
SARAH RUTHERFORD......................Annie Fitzpatrick
HERIONE RUTHERFORD ....Peggy Shay
WENDLE WEEDLE, P.I......................Robert Zukerman
OSWALD, LORD RUTHERFORD ....Marty Allen
BARONESS GRETA VON
    KEEPSEMFRUMFLOPPEN..............Sharon McNight
CAMILLE RUTHERFORD...................Annie Fitzpatrick
CHADWICK STERLING....................Carleton Carpenter

*The character of Ruby Pinkbottom, the brash cockney maid, replaced the character of Quentin Hotchkiss, the astute butler—as is the case with this published version. Also please note that the roles of Sara and Camille Rutherford are written as twins—to be played by the same actress.

Characters
(in order of appearance)

RUBY PINKBOTTOM (A man in a dress)

Devoted maid to the Rutherford family for 15 years. Millicent tolerates Ruby, since William made Ruby a permanent employee of the Rutherford House. The question of the evening is whether Ruby is in the will or not. Ruby gets along famously with Lord Oswald. It is difficult to tell which one is kinkier. Out-going and gregarious, Ruby tickles the funny bones of all those who visit Rutherford House. (Though a drag character, he plays the character as a woman, and comically denies any accusations from guests that he is otherwise.) 35 – 40 years old.

MILLICENT, LADY RUTHERFORD

The domineering, sultry lady of the house. Dressed to the nines, she darts to and fro making sure glasses are full and merriment prevails. Tonight's celebration is a dictate of her last husband, William, Fifth Earl Rutherford (or Earl Rutherford), who wrote in his will that no inheritance would be granted to any of his beneficiaries unless such a celebration occurred for five consecutive years after his death. Millicent married William for his money. She'll do anything to secure it. Her sincerity toward everyone, guests and family, is artificial and forced. There is one exception: Chadwick Sterling—her suave English boyfriend of 8 months with whom she intends to share her part of the inheritance. Millicent is calculating. Morals and ethics don't compete with money and power. The butt of her demanding personality is usually the family maid. Ruby Pinkbottom. Loyalty does not guarantee civility here. She blames Ruby for everything that goes wrong during a social event of hers. For example, if she detects merriment among guests is waning, she sends Ruby to titillate their fancy with fun facts about the history of Rutherford House and details of the interior design. She despises her one daughter Camille, and favors the other, Sarah, even though she has betrayed Sarah, by sleeping with Sarah's fiance Cameron, a secret she has kept from no one except Sarah. If she is confronted with this fact, she simply ad-libs: "I am devoted to Cameron." She is aware that William and the Baroness had a short affair five years ago in Paris, and loathes the Baroness because of it. 47 – 50 years old.

CAMERON WORTHLESTON

Cameron is greedy. He is engaged to Sarah and has a prenuptial agreement which gives him 10% of Sarah's inheritance from William upon marriage. He sleeps with Millicent because of the expensive gifts she buys him. But, he is in love with the Baroness (Trixie) and has decided to assist her in seeking revenge on the Rutherford family. (This, of course, should remain secret until it is divulged in The Resolution.) His father was a nobleman, of sorts, who deserted him and his mother. His mother is a Mary Kay cosmetics salesperson. It is a surprise to everyone, especially Millicent, when the detective discovers that Cameron and Sarah were secretly married, and that he is entitled to part of William's estate. He craves being a jet-setter, and is very smooth, especially with the ladies. However, his social graces are sometimes thwarted by his lack of intelligence. He is tall, attractive and debonaire. 28 years old.

SARAH RUTHERFORD

Millicent's less glamorous twin daughter. She is engaged to marry Cameron Worthleston, but her murder will cancel all plans. She is sweet and naive and a bit awkward. She is unaware that Cameron is involved with Millicent. 24 years old.

HERMIONE RUTHERFORD

Hermione prefers being called Herman because it's less formal. Her reality is warped; her world eccentric; her marbles loose. Being a Rutherford, she has money but no need for it. It's more exciting to panhandle and collect soda cans for reimbursement. She is Lord William's paternal aunt who moved into Rutherford House when her pet cat died. It was a traumatic experience. She hasn't been the same since. She befriends stray cats as if they are lost children. She frequently visits city animal shelters, bringing orphan animals presents. She is totally benevolent and harmless and wants everyone to share in her optimism. She believes in reincarnation and the Great Beyond. Her cats are former relatives and soul mates from former lives. She reads palms and feels psychic vibrations. It was a stipulation in Lord William's will that Hermione be allowed to live in Rutherford House until her death. Millicent is frequently reminded of this. 65 – 70 years old.

WENDLE WEEDLE, P.I.

A dear friend of the Rutherford family who studied at Harvard. He is an eloquent chap who has recently retired as an historian and writer of college textbooks. He is now a part-time private investigator. He solves tonight's case with diligence and impeccable professionalism. Though articulate, he is not so academic that he is off-putting. He is well-read in many areas and is comfortable conversing about everything from Europe's Dark Ages to Los Angeles' latest trends. He is jolly and a zealous socializer. Dressed in safari outfit. 40 – 60 years old.

OSWALD, LORD RUTHERFORD

Oswald is William's younger brother, as he likes to remind people. Bizarre and full of energy, he dresses outrageously. Some family members comment that his wardrobe rivals Liberace's. Because he stands to inherit 10% of William's estate and has already gained total control of the family's tea and tobacco import company, he is not Millicent's favorite person; neither is she his. He blames Millicent for his brother's death, because William died in the throes of love-making which the family has nick-named the "Final Reenactment of Carmen." Not much is known about Oswald's past except that he is a fun-loving man whose reputation as a playboy is as applicable now as it was in his youth. He resides in San Francisco where he runs the family business. He is full of jokes and humorous stories. He enjoys sharing his joie de vivre with people, especially the Baroness, whom he met three years ago when he was traveling in Europe. She was performing in a West Berlin night club. He was not aware of her past involvement with William, but the Baroness knew that Oswald was William's partner in business and that he, too, was responsible for the demise of her family's tea business. He pretends he's blind, walks with a white cane and wears round darkened spectacles. 55 – 60 years old.

BARONESS GRETA VON KEEPSEMFRUMFLOPPEN

This seasoned American cabaret performer is actually Trixie Calahan from Modesto, California (a secret kept until The Resolution). She adopted the persona of the Baroness Greta von Keepsem- fromfloppen when she went to Europe twelve years ago with her cabaret act. Her fabricated past as the Baroness is that she is the heiress of the Keepsemfromfloppen family—the world's largest importer of Westphalian ham. She is a buxom, milky-complexioned cross between Marlene Dietrich and Bette Midler. She speaks with a strong, sometimes cheap, German accent. She gets along with men, but rarely women. She deliberately had an affair with William five years ago in Paris—a rendezvous which began over a glass of Peaches and Cream Liquer at a Montmartre cafe. She informed Millicent of this affair as part of her plot to avenge the Rutherfords for ruining her family's tea business in San Francisco. As Trixie Calahan, she has come this evening to complete the plan she began five years ago. Her partner in crime is her lover, Cameron Worthleston (again kept secret until The Resolution). She is outrageous and fiesty. 35 – 40 years old.

CAMILLE RUTHERFORD (Played by same actress as Sarah)

Millicent's stunning, mysterious twin daughter, Camille is soft-spoken, until provoked. She wants Millicent to like her, but knows that Millicent isn't capable of such emotion. Though not nearly as vindictive as Millicent, her claws are just as long. And when necessary, she brazenly defends herself against Millicent's perfidy. Despite what Millicent says or implies, Camille cared very much for her father, as she does her twin sister Sarah. As the evening progresses, Camille flirts with gentlemen guests, including Chadwick— which of course sets Millicent afire. This is Camille's silent revenge. She neither likes, nor trusts Cameron. 24 years old.

CHADWICK STERLING

An international jet-setter and an established entrepreneur. He owns textile factories in India, Pakistan and Turkey, and has dabbled in and made lots of money from countless other business ventures. Now a multi-millionaire, he lets hired people run his business. He spends his time galavanting around the globe. He met Millicent in Los Angeles 8 months ago at a party for a mutual friend's film opening. It's difficult to decipher whether Millicent isn't just after his money, but something about her long gazes and overt politeness tells us she really loves him. The real test will come tonight when he tells Millicent that his business folded and he is bankrupt. 45 – 55 years old.

Scene

Rutherford House, An elegant townhouse
in New York City

Time

The present

Note: Since dinner may be involved in a production, pacing is very important. To assist the director in timing scenes, playing times are suggested at the beginning of each scene for evening and matinee performances. Also see suggested itinerary at end of play.

Scene 1

7:30 p.m./1:00 p.m.

(MUSIC: Classical – background.

Guests each receive a MURDER AT RUTHERFORD HOUSE dossier and a character assignment. [See MURDER AT RUTHERFORD HOUSE PRODUCTION GUIDE.]

RUBY, MILLICENT, CAMERON and SARAH are cued to work the crowd, asking guests their assigned character names and engaging guests in conversation about their relationships to the Rutherford family. Guest dossiers will be available at rehearsals for performers to review and familiarize themselves with the guests that they should know i.e., Millicent went on a cruise last year with Ty Tanic, the ship builder.

Millicent has invited the all guests here tonight per a clause in William's will which requires Millicent to throw a party in his honor on the anniversary of his death for five consecutive years. She would forfeit her inheritance (30% of William's entire estate) if she did not abide by William's wish. Tonight is the fifth and final celebration. Tomorrow she plans to be a very wealthy woman. Once most of the guests have arrived, MILLICENT darts to and fro socializing and flirting with the male guests. Occasionally she deposits ashes from her cigarette in William's urn and jokes about it. SARAH and CAMERON talk to guests about their upcoming wedding, among other things.)

7:40/1:10

(HERMIONE is cued to run through the crowd giggling. SHE then exits. After 30 seconds, SARAH exits, then CAMERON. This is RUBY's cue to begin dusting guests with her fluffy duster.

MUSIC: out.)

RUBY. You know, from the evening dusk to the morning sun, this maid's work is never done. Oh sorry, sir, I missed a spot on your lapel. This is my fuzzy. I call him quickie 'cause he fuzzes faster than any fuzzy around (*Squeals.*)

MILLICENT. Ruby, you were asked to stay in the east wing of the mansion during tonight's celebration.

RUDY. Oh yeah, you're right. I was. Sorry about that your (*Curtseys.*) majesty, your (*Curtseys.*) highness, (*Backs away.*) your royal pain in the dust pan.

MILLICENT. Ruby!

RUBY. Don't go gettin' your ruffles all wrinkled.

MILLICENT. You're dismissed!
RUBY. (*Stalks Millicent.*) Oh don't dismiss me, your ladyship. (*Threatening.*) You don't want to dismiss me. I know too much. Remember!
MILLICENT. You may stay.
RUBY. Poor Lady Millicent, the city scene's settin' her silly. Not me. I'm glad the Rutherfords decided to take me to their uptown residence. Us West End girls need a break once and a while. (*To a gentleman guest.*) All right, who wants to be the first to break me in? (*Squeals.*)

(*RUBY squeals, WENDLE enters, chasing imaginary butterfly with net.*)

MUSIC CUE No. 1

WENDLE. Come back here. Come back here I say. Darn it! Now, you won't get away from me you writhing ... fluttering ... thing you.

(*WENDLE swings to catch butterfly, misses and hits RUBY in the behind. With her back toward WENDLE, she has been writhing to his words with "oohs and ahhs," thinking he is referring to her.*)

RUBY. Oh mister, you know me so well, and we haven't even met.
WENDLE. My dear ... lady ... I am Wendle Weedle.

RUBY. (*Extends hand.*) Ruby Pinkbottom at your service. So, what're ya doin' after this shindig?

WENDLE. I beg your pardon?

RUBY. What'd'ya say you and me polish the Big Apple?

MILLICENT. Ruby, off with you!

RUBY. Yeah. Yeah. (*Takes Wendle's net.*) Check your net? Ooh, full of holes ... I'll mend it for you. (*Exits with net.*)

WENDLE. Thank you. Millicent, so sorry I'm late. I was tracking this rare New York butterfly, the Koch's Nonelectus, which gave me the run of my life.

MILLICENT. Yes, well join the festivities, won't you?

WENDLE. Jolly good idea.

MUSIC CUE NO. 2

(*WENDLE joins the crowd. SARAH reenters.*)

SARAH. Mother, I can't seem to find my diamond bracelet—the one Daddy bought me.

MILLICENT. Did you look in your jewelry box?

SARAH. Yes. It's not there. It's not anywhere in my room.

MILLICENT. Oh, you're hopeless. How could you lose a diamond bracelet? (*To a guest.*) Can you believe she lost diamonds? (*To Sarah.*) Come with me. I'll help you find it.

(*MILLICENT takes SARAH through the crowd on route to upstairs. They bicker as they exit. SARAH is embarrassed, ad-libbing "Oh Mother, not so loud," etc. OSWALD, LORD RUTHERFORD enters full of energy, with a suitcase and a shopping bag. He is outrageously dressed and decorated with much jewelry. Dark glasses cover his eyes. He carries a "blind person's" cane, vigorously tapping it as he walks.*)

RUBY. Lord Oswald.
OSWALD. (*Feeling Ruby's face.*) Hello, Ruby.
RUBY. Shall I announce you sir?
OSWALD. Of course.
RUBY. (*Rings bell.*) Ladies and gentlemen, Oswald, Lord Rutherford.
OSWALD. Thank you. (*Walking through the crowd.*) Where's the high priestess?
RUBY. I beg your pardon.
OSWALD. Millicent.
MILLICENT. (*Enters.*) Oswald, you're on time this year.
OSWALD. I was hoping the shock would kill you.
MILLICENT. Staying long?
OSWALD. Long enough to take care of business.
MILLICENT. (*Sly.*) Oh yes, the will. (*They exchange a wry glance.*)

MUSIC CUE NO. 4

MILLICENT. Tell me Oswald, how was your trip to Savannah?

OSWALD. Profitable.

MILLICENT. Who has Rutherford Tea and Spice destroyed this month?

OSWALD. That is no longer your business.

MILLICENT. Yes. You're in the front room this year. I'll have Ruby take up your bags.

OSWALD. (*Feeling around, searching for the urn.*) Where's my dear brother?

MILLICENT. Over here.

OSWALD. Where?

MILLICENT. (*Louder.*) Over here.

OSWALD. Over where?

MILLICENT. (*Crude Cockney.*) Over 'ere.

OSWALD. Millicent, (*Touches arm of chair.*) You've lost weight.

MILLICENT. Tell me Oswald, why are you wearing those ridiculous dark glasses?

OSWALD. This year I'm blind.

MUSIC CUE NO. 5

RUBY. Blind?! Lord Oswald.

OSWALD. Yes, remember last year it was the heartbreak of psoriasis, and the year before that it was shingles. Oh Ruby, fetch my bag. I brought you a present.

(*RUBY fetches the bag. OSWALD continues.*)

OSWALD. You're going to love it. It's anatomically correct and battery operated.

(*RUBY holds the bag open for OSWALD. He pulls out a garishly decorated bra.*)

OSWALD. I haven't used that in a long time. (*Puts it back.*) It was always a bust. (*Pulls out revolver.*
RUBY. Lord Oswald, what's that?
OSWALD. It's to protect myself from Millicent. (*Picks up gift-wrapped box and hands it to Ruby.*) Here it is. The key to a young woman's...
RUBY. (*Embarrassed, puts hand over OSWALD's mouth.*) Heart. Come on, Uncle Oswald. I'll help you upstairs.
OSWALD. (*Leaving.*) You do know how to use one, don't you?

MUSIC CUE NO. 6

(*They exit. CAMERON descends the stairs. He is looking for SARAH.*)

CAMERON. Millicent, Millicent, have you seen Sarah? There's a telephone call for her.
MILLICENT. I didn't hear the telephone ring.
CAMERON. It was on the upstairs line.

MILLICENT. The upstairs line hasn't worked for weeks.

CAMERON. (*Stammering.*) It ... um ... was repaired this morning.

MILLICENT. Sarah's somewhere getting ready.

CAMERON. Thank you. (*Exits.*)

MILLICENT. (*To audience.*) I am devoted to Cameron.

MUSIC CUE NO. 7

(*MILLICENT starts to follow CAMERON, then notices the BARONESS GRETA VON KEEPSEMFRUMFLOPPEN entering. MILLICENT stands aside.*)

BARONESS. Ya! I am here. Introduce me, please.

RUBY. Ladies and gentle ...

BARONESS. (*Hands RUBY her phony invitation.*) A proper introduction, please.

RUBY. (*Rings her bell.*) Ladies and gentlemen, your attention please. It gives me great honor to welcome to Rutherford House this (number) day of (month) from Baden Baden, West Germany, the Baroness Greta von Keepsenfrumfloppen (*Pronounced "flawpen."*).

BARONESS. Floppen! (*Pronounced "flōpen."*)

RUBY. (*Corrects the pronunciation.*) The Baroness Greta Von Keepsemfrumfloppen.

BARONESS. Floppen! (*Pronounced "flōpen."*)

RUBY. (*Corrects the pronunciation.*) The Baroness Greta Von Keepsemfrumfloppen.

BARONESS. Das is better. (*Walking through crowd.*) Ya, I am że Baroness Greta von Keepsemfrumfloppen: vell-traveled, vell-liked *und* vell-endowed. I, like all of you am here in honor of ze late Wilhelm Ruserford, who died five years ago tonight on ze pink satin sheets of ze king-sized bed upstairs. How do I know ze color of ze sheets? Wilhelm vas patron of my endowments. (*Laughs.*) Vhere is ze grieving vidow? Opening a sviss bank account?

(*Note: The above passage is written phonetically. This is an example of the Baroness' accent, which should be applied to the rest of her dialogue.*)

MILLICENT. (*Comes forward.*) Greta, I don't believe you were invited to tonight's celebration.

BARONESS. I wouldn't have missed this for all the tea in the Rutherford empire.

MILLICENT. (*Referring to Baroness' dress.*) Greta, did your pet racoon die?

BARONESS. Oh Millicent, you are in rare form tonight.

MILLICENT. Better to be in rare form than inflated form.

BARONESS. Millicent, your bite is unusually venomous this evening. Been cuddling a cobra?

MILLICENT. (*Sharp.*) Stay out of my personal life.

BARONESS. (*Emphatically.*) Dear Millicent, I have just begin to rattle the bones which will destroy the Rutherford empire.

MILLICENT. I'm warning you.

BARONESS. Don't warn me. I got two words for you, and they ain't Happy Birthday. (*Briskly exits.*)

RUBY. (*Runs to console Millicent.*) Oh your Ladyship, don't you mind that dirty ole windbag.

MILLICENT. Ruby, introduce me.

RUBY. (*Rings bell.*) Ladies and gentlemen, the lady of the house would like to speak with you. I give you Millicent, Lady Rutherford.

MILLICENT. Thank you. Ladies and gentlemen, I want to thank you all for coming this evening. As you know, this is the fifth and final dinner party celebrating the anniversary of my husband William's death—a celebration dear William requested in his will. It was five years ago tonight, my husband died while in the throes of passionate love-making. We had just returned from the opera, *Carmen* ...

MUSIC CUE NO. 8: ("The Habanera" from *Carmen. It starts slow and increases in tempo and intensity under MILLICENT.*)

MILLICENT. William wanted to reenact it ... live ... under the sheets, *he* wanted to be Carmen. Well, he grabbed a rose from the vase next to the bed, stuck it between his teeth, and thus started the seduction. Part way in the "Habanera," something in him began to give way. The tempo increased. William could not keep up. And on the final chord ...

(*MUSIC: plunk chord.*)

MILLICENT. ... he died.

(*SARAH enters on "died" and screams. Two gunshots ring out. She stumbles with choreographed movement and dies.*)

MUSIC CUE NO. 9: (*MRH Theme.*)

WENDLE. (*Entering.*) Gunshots! Ladies and gentlemen, I heard gunshots. (*Sees SARAH, then runs for stretcher and sheet.*

(*MUSIC - MRH Theme - swells.*)

CAMERON. (*Entering.*) Sarah! (*Runs to her, then consoles MILLICENT, as they both weep over SARAH's body.*)
RUBY. Oh, oh, dial 411, dial 411. No, that's information. Dial 911.

(*WENDLE and CAMERON load SARAH onto the stretcher, cover her with the sheet and carry her out. The following dialogue is under this.*)

RUBY. Oh, she was so young.
MILLICENT. So pure.
RUBY. So young, carry on!

MUSIC CUE NO. 10: (*MRH Theme.*)
(*Segues into background music.*)

(*Waiters enter in procession and serve Course #1.
MILLICENT and CAMERON sit together.
MUSIC: Background
Note: No break here during brunch!*

Scene 2

8:05 p.m.

(*MUSIC: Out.*)

WENDLE. Ladies and gentlemen, such a tragedy that on the evening of the fifth anniversary of her father's death, poor Sarah Rutherford should perish. Allow me to introduce myself. I am Wendle Weedle, B.A. M.A., Ph.D., P.I. Last year I assisted the New York City Police Department in several noteworthy cases. As an expert on the medieval period, it would seem to me that such dark ages have descended upon us once again. Yes, the crime at hand is a most disturbing, heinous one. And I will do everything in my power to right this evil deed. But I need your assistance. Now, who was away from the cocktail reception at the time of the murder?

MUSIC CUE NO. 11 (*Mysterious Roll.*)

(*MILLICENT and CAMERON stand and look around. CAMILLE enters in a dress much more elegant than her twin sister, Sarah was wearing.*)

CAMILLE. I was.
MILLICENT. There's your murderer, Wendle. It all fits ... The shooting lessons last spring, the resentment toward her twin sister Sarah and of course, William's will.
CAMILLE. Keep out of this, Millicent.
MILLICENT. Oh no you don't—you're not getting away with anything this time. Your father's not around to protect you like he did all those years.
CAMILLE. It's not time to play the wicked witch.
MILLICENT. (*A la Snow White's evil queen.*) Wicked! Who are you calling wicked?

(*They argue.*)

WENDLE. All right, ladies, stifle. This is getting us nowhere. Now, Camille, where were you when the shots were fired?
CAMILLE. I was in the upstairs ladies' room.
WENDLE. Did you hear the gunshots?

CAMILLE. Yes I did.
MILLICENT. Then why are you appearing only now?
CAMILLE. Because, Mommie dearest, there are some things you just can't interrupt.
MILLICENT. I will never forgive you if you are responsible for my daughter's death.
CAMILLE. I'm your daughter, too.
MILLICENT. Unfortunately.
WENDLE. Camille, please sit down. (MUSIC CUE NO. 12) (*Sits.*) Now, ladies and gentlemen, was anyone else ...

MUSIC CUE NO. 13

(*A loud banging is heard from inside a nearby closet.*)

WENDLE. My goodness, what was that?
MILLICENT. What?

(*The banging continues, accompanied by raucous laughter.*)

WENDLE. That.
BARONESS. (*Steps out.*) Ve vant to be alone!

(*She abruptly closes the door. OSWALD steps out, shirt untucked and laughing. BARONESS joins OSWALD back in.*)

WENDLE. Oswald, come out of there. Come up both of you.

(They obey.)

BARONESS. *(Walking.)* It was so much fun noshing with Ozzie in the closet.
WENDLE. Oswald, why don't you introduce me to your friend?
BARONESS. What! You missed my introduction earlier, maybe? I am the Baroness Greta von Keepsemfrumfloppen.
WENDLE. *(Writing in his pad.)* The Baroness Greta von Keepsemfrumfloppen *("Flawpen")*, huh?
BARONESS & OSWALD. Floppen! *("Flōpen")*
WENDLE. Ah, yes—floppen. Now, what were you two doing in the closet while a murder took place? Surely you heard the gunshots.
OSWALD. I was giving the Baroness a tour of the house, and she was giving me ...
BARONESS. Ozzie, darling, let me explain. You see ... wait a minute. What is your name?
WENDLE. I am Wendle Weedle, PI.
BARONESS. Wendle Weedle ... how cute. What is PI?
WENDLE. Private investigator.
BARONESS. *(Taken back.)* Aah! Gestapo! *(Beat.)* Anyway your friend and I were engaged in a very popular German game which I used to play with all the American soldiers stationed in

West Germany. It's called (*Rotates hips.*) "Sink the Bismark" (*Thrusts hips forward.*)

MUSIC CUE NO. 14 (*Chord.*)

OSWALD. My bomb-bay doors were open, and I was going in for the attack ... (*He demonstrates.*)

BARONESS. (*Laughing.*) American men are so ...

BARONESS & OSWALD. (*Dancing in place.*) Vunderful, 'S Marvelous. (*Their laughter builds.*)

MILLICENT. (*Curt.*) Including my dear William. Right, Greta?

BARONESS. Millicent, your dear William was no common soldier. He was a (*Salutes.*) five star general.

MILLICENT. Greta, you're not an invited guest. Why don't you just leave?

OSWALD. Millicent, please.

BARONESS. I will leave when we ...

BARONESS & OSWALD. (*With movement.*) Sink the Bismark.

MUSIC CUE NO. 15

(*Two gunshots ring out. With gun in hand, HERMIONE enters flustered. CAMILLE runs to her aid.*)

HERMIONE. Those damn pigeons. They just won't stand still.

CAMILLE. Aunt Herman, what are you doing?

HERMIONE. Trying to shoot pigeons. Sarah told me she wanted poultry for dinner.

CAMILLE. Sarah is dead, Aunt Herman.

HERMIONE. Why didn't she tell me? I wouldn't have stood outside all that time shooting at things that won't stand still.

(*HERMIONE drifts into her own world. CAMILLE takes the gun from HERMIONE and gives it to RUBY, then sits.*)

WENDLE. Is this your aunt, Millicent?

OSWALD. She's my aunt. A Rutherford. Her name is Hermione, but she likes to be called Herman.

WENDLE. Herman?

HERMIONE. Yes. What is it? I'm sorry there'll be no poultry for dinner tonight. The damn things won't stand still. Millicent, dear, when you see Sarah, will you tell her there'll be no poultry tonight?

MILLICENT. I'll do that Aunt Herman.

HERMIONE. I must find something else for dinner. I'll be back shortly. (*She exits giggling.*)

WENDLE. Does Hermione have a permit for that gun?

RUBY. If you'll excuse me, Hermione doesn't have a permit to be loose on the street, much less to carry a gun. You see, Aunt Hermione's cheese has fallen off its cracker.

WENDLE. Thank you, Ruby. Ladies and gentlemen, I have some information to gather and several phone calls to make. Remember, until the murderer is apprehended, you are all suspects. At this time please open the first, and only the first, seal on your dossiers. And now ... finish your fruit!

For Brunch

... Ruby has a few welcome words.

RUBY. Ladies and gentlemen, brunch is served.

MUSIC CUE NO. 16:
(Segue to classical background.)

(WENDLE exits. CAMERON sits with MILLICENT for a while. Then he excuses himself, saying he doesn't feel well, after all that has happened. He exits. All other characters present work the crowd, i.e. socialize table-to-table. Guests open first clue: a set of limericks which needs ordering. When unscrambled, it reads:

THERE IS AN UNLIKELY DUET
WHO LIVES A SECRET WELL-KEPT
EACH HAS A CALL
TO PERPETRATE ONE FALL

DECEIT IS AN ART AT WHICH BOTH ARE ADEPT

WITH HEIGHTENED MALEVOLENCE AND GREED
A VOW OF DESTRUCTION THEY WOULD HEED
THEIR PLOT WELL-PLANNED
THY DUO WOULD STAND
AGAINST THE CLAN OF AMORAL CREED

(Waiters clear Course #. 1.
When cued:)

RUBY. Ladies and gentlemen, it give me great pleasure to announce *(Rings bell.)* The second course is served.

Scene 3

8:25 p.m.

(WENDLE enters. MUSIC: Out.)

WENDLE. Ladies and gentlemen, I just got off the phone with the local hospital. I was informed that Sarah Rutherford was pronounced dead on arrival from multiple gunshot wounds to the chest. A ballistics report from the police department has not yet been completed, but doctors are fairly certain that the bullets were from a .22 calibre handgun. If you know guns, you know that a .22 is easily fired by a man or a woman. Now I've searched the upstairs for clues, since this is where I believe the killer watched Sarah and then followed her as she made her descent downstairs. I found this. [MUSIC CUE NO. 17] (*Presents notes and reads.*) It reads: "Dear Sarah, I can't stand it any longer. You must brake your engagement immediately. I'm warning you. I'll take drastic measures if you don't comply with my request. Signed, Larry Looselips. (*A Guest.*)

Mr. Looselips, would you please stand? I ask you to stand because you were having a relationship with an engaged woman, Sarah Rutherford. Were you not? (*Guest answers.*) Her engagement to Cameron obviously angered you very much. Were you so angry that you killed her? (*Guest answers.*) Did you know her fiance, Cameron? (*Guest answers.*) What did you mean when you said you would take drastic measures if she didn't break off her engagement? (*Guest answers. Then WENDLE looks around the room.*) By the way, where is Cameron? Camille, have you seen Cameron?

MUSIC CUE NO. 18

CAMILLE. (*Stands.*) Check Millicent's bedroom.
MILLICENT. Jealous dear?

CAMILLE. I'm not jealous. I'm disgusted. And where's your Cassanova du jour, Chadwick?

MILLICENT. He's due in tomorrow.

OSWALD. My, for a loose woman, she's got a real tight schedule.

MILLICENT. That's it! I'll take no more of your condescending remarks, not in my house. Get out, both of you.

CAMILLE. What's the matter Millicent? The truth too much outside the bedroom? It wasn't enough to undermine Sarah, your own daughter, by sleeping with her fiance. Now you have to embarrass her?

MILLICENT. Camille, sit down.

CAMILLE. No, you let me finish. Sarah's no longer here to be victim to your selfishness, but I am. And this is where it stops. I am not going to continue being the brunt of your derogatory remarks. I'm warning you—keep it up and you'll be sorry.

(They stare each other down.)

WENDLE. Ladies, please. This isn't helping us find the murderer.

BARONESS. No, but it's better than *Dynasty*.

MILLICENT. Baroness, don't start.

OSWALD. Millicent, sit down and leave the poor child alone.

BARONESS. (*Rises.*) Ya, sit down and chew your lettuce.

MILLICENT. Greta, a woman with your past should think twice about telling me what to do. All I need do is drop a few fun facts about you and William, and we'll soon see who walks out of here with her tail between her legs.

BARONESS. (*Sexy.*) Ooh, sounds vunderful.

MILLICENT. You think I'm kidding do you?

BARONESS. Go on, Millicent. (*Strikes masculine pose.*) Make my day.

MILLICENT. I will, Greta. I promise.

WENDLE. (*Blows whistle.*) Ladies, we must have decorum. Now, please sit down and ...

(*HERMIONE excitedly runs in with a ransom note in hand. MILLICENT and BARONESS sit.*)

HERMIONE. Mr. Weedle, Mr. Weedle, look what I found. Look what I found. (*She hands note to him.*)

WENDLE. Let me see it. Ladies and gentlemen, it's a ransom note.

MUSIC CUE NO. 19

WENDLE. It's made from magazine cut-outs. It reads: "Comply or he'll die." Where did you find it?

HERMIONE. It was in the parlor. Did you know that while in there William spoke to me? He said that there'd be a tempest in the house tonight

and that we should all beware. I heard him say it. I heard him say it ...
WENDLE. Miss Rutherford ...
HERMIONE. Herman.
WENDLE. Herman, did you see anyone leave this note?
HERMIONE. No, but this handkerchief was next to the note. It's a lovely little handkerchief.

(*HERMIONE presents the handkerchief to WENDLE. It is a white linen handkerchief with "C.A.M." embroidered on it. CAMILLE sits HERMIONE down.*)

WENDLE. This handkerchief has initials embroidered on it. (*To a guest.*) Would you be so kind as to tell me what those initials are.
GUEST. C.A.M.
WENDLE. C.A.M. Camille, is this yours?

MUSIC CUE NO. 20

CAMILLE. (*Stand to look at it.*) Is that mine? (*Beat.*) No.
WENDLE. Does anyone recognize it?
OSWALD. I don't recognize anything.
BARONESS. It's Cameron's.
MILLICENT. How do you know?
BARONESS. He blew his nose with it earlier.
WENDLE. Millicent, can you confirm that it belongs to Cameron?
MILLICENT. Yes, it's his.

WENDLE. Well, ladies and gentlemen, it seems we've a kidnapping on our hands—that of the murder victim's fiance, Cameron Worthleston.

MUSIC CUE NO. 21 *Chadwick's Entrance*

(*CHADWICK gallantly enters carrying a handbag.*)

CHADWICK. Millicent, Millicent. it's me. I'm back early. (*Looks around.*) You have guests.

(*MUSIC: Out.*)

MILLICENT. (*Approaches him.*) Chadwick.
CHADWICK. Millicent, what's going on?
MILLICENT. It's an anniversary party.
CHADWICK. For whom? Sarah and Cameron aren't even married yet.
MILLICENT. Darling, I'm afraid Sarah is dead and Cameron has been kidnapped.
WENDLE. And you, sir, are now a suspect.
MILLICENT. So sorry, darling.
CHADWICK. Suspect? You are wrong. I just arrived in a taxi from the airport.
WENDLE. Which airport?
CHADWICK. Newark. Why?
OSWALD. Wendle, never trust anyone who flies into Newark.
HERMIONE. I fly into Newark every morning. I fly in from all over the universe.

Sometimes from Brooklyn, other times from Jupiter.
CHADWICK. Just what is going on?
BARONESS. It's the reunion of the Addams family.
CHADWICK. Anniversary ... reunion ... come, come. Millicent, is this an elaborate prank to welcome me into the family?
HERMIONE. (*Runs to CHADWICK.*) I knew William would come back. (*Hugs CHADWICK.*) Welcome back, William. I've been waiting for you. Welcome!
CHADWICK. Madam, desist. Millicent!
MILLICENT. (*As if to say "Let me explain."*) Chadwick ...
HERMIONE. (*Hugs him again.*) William!
WENDLE. Ladies and gentlemen ... Please! I've a serious investigation to conduct.

(*HERMIONE sits.*)

WENDLE. Now, sir, what is your full name?
CHADWICK. I am Chadwick Sterling. Who are you?
WENDLE. Wendle Weedle, P.I.
CHADWICK. (*Laughs.*) Ha, ha, ha ... Wendle Weedle. Are you part of the jest?
WENDLE. Sir, I'll have you know I am in charge here, in charge of a major murder/kidnapping case in which you are a prime suspect.

CHADWICK. What a preposterous accusation. I barely just arrived from London.

MILLICENT. But Chadwick, why are you back early?

MUSIC CUE NO. 22
(Mysterious trill—Cue for CAMERON to dial phone, when phone call is live.)

CHADWICK. I'll explain ... later.

(CHADWICK exits to deposit his things. Phone rings. RUBY enters. If phone call is live and phone does not ring, RUBY anticipates entrance, to have phone in hand for next line. If call is not live, RUBY carries a prop phone on a tray.)

RUBY. *(Picks up phone.)* Hello, Rutherford House. For whom are you calling? Ladies and gentlemen, I have a call for a Ms. Enny Price. *(A Guest.)*

(RUBY hands ENNY the phone (if live). CAMERON is on the other end. If phone is a prop, WENDLE intercepts, takes the phone and delivers Enny's lines.)

CAMERON. *(On phone.)* Hello, Enny. This is Cameron Worthleston.

(RUBY prompts ENNY to tell who it is.)

BARONESS. Who is it? Who is it?
ENNY. Cameron.
BARONESS. Cameron!

MUSIC CUE NO. 23 -*Chord*

CAMILLE. Cameron!

(*MUSIC: Chord.*)

MILLICENT. Cameron!

(*MUSIC: Chord.*)

(*WENDLE scurries over to ENNY and asks all the appropriate questions to get all of the information out, if she doesn't offer it.*)

CAMERON. (*On phone.*) I've been kidnapped. They're holding me at gunpoint. My kidnapper's won't release me alive unless you deliver all of the jewels and cash of all the guests at tonight's party in a shopping bag to Bethesda Fountain in Central Park in fifteen minutes. Make sure to include Millicent's 10 carat diamond ring.
MILLICENT. What?! (*Grabs ring.*) Oh what a shame he has to die.

(*CAMERON screams in agony. WENDLE grabs the phone.*)

WENDLE. Hello, hello, hello. The line has gone dead.

MUSIC CUE NO. 24

MILLICENT. Oh Wendle, perhaps there's still hope, if we can get enough jewels and cash from our guests. (*Runs to him.*) Wendle, do something.

WENDLE. Ladies and gentlemen, while I'm not one that condones conceding to the wishes of terrorists and kidnappers, let me ask you, who here would be willing to give up their jewels and cash to bring Cameron back?

MUSIC CUE NO. 25

RUBY. (*Passes through the crowd with tray.*) Donations, donations (*Ad-libs until she reaches BARONESS.*)

(*MUSIC: Out.*)

BARONESS. I will give all that I've got. I think that all the ladies should do the same.

(*She puts her bracelet on the tray. RUBY takes jewel to WENDLE who examines it.*)

WENDLE. I don't think that the Baroness' cubic zirconia will get Cameron back.

BARONESS. Watch it, Weedle, or you're gonna be wearing those jewels.

WENDLE. No offense, Baroness, but facts are facts. Now I'm gong to call the local authorities and see if they have had any word from Cameron Worthleston or his kidnappers. In the interim (*Beat.*) carry on. (*Exits.*)

MUSIC CUE NO. 26
(Segue to classical background.)

(*CHADWICK reenters. MILLICENT takes him table-to-table and introduces him to guests. All other characters work the tables. Waiters clear second course. When the main course is ready, RUBY is cued. MUSIC: Out.*)

RUBY. Ladies and gentlemen, you each received a piece of bribe money to bribe your favorite suspect. Feel free to use it at any time. And now I bubble over with joy to announce (*Rings bell.*) The main course is served.

MUSIC CUE NO. 27

(Then classical background.
Waiters enter in a procession with the main course. HERMIONE exits with urn. BARONESS receives a pot of hot water into which she puts one of her Pacific tea bags. With tea in hand, label hanging off the saucer, she works the tables.

Guests have each received a piece of "bribe money." Throughout the remainder of the evening, they can bribe any one character with this money. Actor's "Bribe Clues" are as follows:)

MILLICENT	I get what I want; others kill for it.
BARONESS	Oswald is as power hungry as Wilhelm was. My father told me this.
OSWALD	All's fair in love and tea.
CAMILLE	Earlier, I saw the Baroness alone with Cameron.
CAMERON	In business and in pleasure, I take what I can get.
HERMIONE	A son is a son 'til he gets him a wife, a daughter is a daughter all of her life.
CHADWICK	Aunt Hermione speaks words of wisdom.
RUBY	Blondes have more fun.

Scene 4

When the entree is underway, OSWALD is cued to make the evening's toast.
MUSIC: Out.

OSWALD. (*Facing sideways.*) Ladies and gentlemen, may I have your attention, please ...

MURDER AT RUTHERFORD HOUSE   43

BARONESS. (*Turns him forward.*) There, Ozzie.

OSWALD. Ladies and gentlemen, as you may know Fanueil Hall marketplace is the third most visited pleasure spot in America. I give you the second, Millicent, Lady (*Coughs.*) Rutherford. (*Sits in SR seat.*)

MILLICENT. (*Stands.*) Thank you, Oswald. Thank you all. On behalf of the Rutherford family, welcome again.

MUSIC CUE NO. 28 (*MRH Theme*)

MILLICENT. Today we lay the ashes of my dearly departed husband to rest once and for all. It was the will of my husband Lord William that all of you, *his* friends be invited here and that his will be read tonight. At this time I give you my husband's brother who ... (*Build with anger.*) ... so expeditiously took over the helm of the Rutherford tea and spice empire when my husband died. (*Sighs and regains composure.*) To make a toast, Oswald.

(*MUSIC: Out.*)

OSWALD. (*Stands.*) Thank you, Millicent. Ladies and gentlemen, I would like to propose a toast. Please raise your glasses. (*He and the guests raise their glasses.*)

MUSIC CUE NO. 29

OSWALD. (*Bombastic.*) In 1820 when our great, great grandfather Charles Peter William, first Earl Rutherford, put the first Rutherford tea bag into a teacup, little did we know that even today, 169 years later, the Rutherford name would still be in hot water worldwide. Yes, we've had to step on a few toes to get what we've got. But from London to Liverpool, from San Francisco to Stuyvesant Square, Rutherford is a household word.

MILLICENT. Oh get on with it, Oswald.

OSWALD. Those of us remaining will always remember my brother William, who guided us for 25 years at the helm of the Rutherford empire. (*Big.*) A toast to Lord Rutherford.

ALL. (*Toast and sing.*) Lord Rutherford.

MUSIC CUE NO. 30

(*OSWALD gulps his wine and starts gagging as if poisoned.*)

MUSIC CUE NO. 31

MILLICENT. Oswald, what is it?

(*MUSIC: Out.*)

OSWALD. 1979. A very bad year.

MUSIC CUE NO. 32

(*HERMIONE enters embracing William's urn. She speaks to William as she carries him through the ballroom.*)

HERMIONE. Look at all your friends, William. They've all come to help you celebrate. (*Pointing out guests.*) There's Lord Byron and Lady Chatterly. Look, Mother Goose just laid an egg and Humpty Dumpty is about to fall. Watch out, Humpty. (*A beat.*) William, do you remember that song I used to sing to you when you were a little boy? Would you like me to sing it to you now? (*Takes the lid off the urn and listens inside.*) You would!

(*She sings a French ballad in a lilting falsetto. After the first "A," MILLICENT grows embarrassed.*)

MILLICENT. (*Stands.*) Chadwick, stop her. She's causing a scene.
CHADWICK. She's not harming anyone.
MILLICENT. She's destroying me. Look at her.

MUSIC CUE NO. 33

CHADWICK approaches HERMIONE, takes the urn, puts it down, and by the second "A" of the song, he eases into a waltz with her. He waltzes her through the room and to her seat. During the waltz, CHADWICK motions to RUBY, who enters with HERMIONE's sedative in hand, which is contained in an oversized medicine bottle, and a large spoon. During the following, CHADWICK discreetly retrieves the urn and places it on a pedestal set in the room, where it shall remain for the rest of the evening. He then sits.

RUBY. It's all right, Mr. Sterling. I'll take it from here. Aunt Hermione, it's time for our sedative.
HERMIONE. Do I have to?
RUBY. Yes, you do. Here comes the plane. Open up the hangar.

(*HERMIONE winces a bit, but puts up no fight and takes the sedative, then barks at RUBY.*)

BARONESS. Ruby, when you're done, pass that stuff around. We went to party, too.

(*RUBY exits. WENDLE enters.*)

WENDLE. Ladies and gentlemen, may I have your attention please. [I was just informed by a member of the staff that written on the ladies' room mirror in lipstick is the message: "I've waited 15 years for this."] (*The preceding dialogue in brackets is eliminated if the message appears in the performance space and not on the ladies' room mirror.*) I regret being the bearer of bad tidings. However, some time has passed, and we've not heard a word from Cameron Worthleston or his kidnappers. The local authorities have turned up nothing, and I regret to say that your unwillingness to give up your jewels and a sufficient amount of cash may have cost Cameron his life.

MUSIC CUE NO. 34 (*Prophetic underscore.*)

(*HERMIONE approaches a male guest "oohing." She is in a trance. She puts her hands on the sides of his head to communicate with the great beyond.*)

HERMIONE.
If what you say is true,
All killing tonight is through;
Except for one who is in this room,
No one else will cause gloom or doom.
    BARONESS. (*Taps glass with spoon.*) Hermione, Hermione, come back.

(*MUSIC: Out.*)

    HERMIONE. Where was I?
    OSWALD. K-Mart.
    HERMIONE. Oh. How was it?
    OSWALD. Cheap. Now sit down before we mark you down.
    HERMIONE. Oh, yes.

(*She sits. MILLICENT stands.*)

MILLICENT. Wendle, I think it's time for the reading of the will.

MUSIC CUE NO. 35

(*WENDLE takes off the lid of the urn, which sits on the pedestal, and removes the will which is taped to the inside.*)

WENDLE. Would the following beneficiaries please come forward: Millicent, Lady Rutherford. (*Sits in SL chair.*)

MUSIC CUE NO. 36

WENDLE. Oswald, Lord Rutherford. (*Sits in SR chair.*)

MUSIC CUE NO. 37

WENDLE. Camille Rutherford. (*Sits on arm of SL chair.*)

MUSIC CUE NO. 38

WENDLE. Hermione Rutherford. (*Stands SL of Millicent.*)

MUSIC CUE NO. 39

WENDLE. And ... Miss Ruby Pinkbottom.

MUSIC CUE NO. 40

(RUBY runs forward, yelping as though she has been selected as a game show contestant, squeezes self in between CAMILLE and OSWALD, forcing OSWALD to stand. HERMIONE takes blow bubbles out of purse and blows them intermittently, so as not to upstage the reading.
LIGHTS: house dim, BENEFICIARIES and WENDLE lit in spots.)

WENDLE. The following is the Last Will and Testament of William Edward Charles, Fifth Earl Rutherford.

I, William Edward Charles Rutherford, being of sound mind and character on this first day of June, Nineteen Hundred and Eighty-two do hereby make my Last Will and Testament. Upon the occasion of my death, I bequeath the following: to my younger brother Oswald, I leave all my business holdings, including my fifty percent of stock in Rutherford Tea and Spice Imports. As for my monetary wealth, I place the following stipulation: upon my death my beneficiaries must for five consecutive years on the anniversary of my unfortunate demise have a celebration in my honor with a guest list comprised of the following names (*Aside.*) I don't think I'll read this. We're all on it. (*Continuing.*) I, William Edward Charles Rutherford, will be in attendance at these celebrations, as my ashes must remain in the Rutherford mansion in perpetuity to remind my family and friends of me. On the day following the eve of the fifth and final celebration, my monetary wealth, estimated this year at Two Hundred and Twenty-six million dollars ...

(*OSWALD energetically taps cane on floor. ALL react.*)

WENDLE. ... will be divided as follows: to my beloved wife, Millicent, (*She stands.*) I leave thirty percent of my fortune provided that she follows my lawyers instructions and does not remarry for five years after my death. Dear Millicent, little do you realize that I have *always* known how much you *really* care for me. (*Sits.*) To my two beautiful daughters, Sarah and Camille (*CAMILLE stands.*) I leave sixty percent of my wealth to divide between you. (*Sits.*) To my brother, Oswald, (*He stands.*) Ten percent of my fortune to support his curious and kinky extracurricular activities.

BARONESS. Ja Wol! (*Pronounced "ya vol."*)

(*OSWALD sits.*)

WENDLE. To my dear Aunt Hermione, (*She steps forward.*) I leave the run of the mansion where she can reside to be comfortably supported by my wife for the rest of *this* lifetime.

HERMIONE. Ha, ha, ha!

WENDLE. Should any of my beneficiaries, provided they are not married, precede the others in death ...

(BENEFICIARIES lean forward.)

WENDLE. ...their share shall be distributed to the first remaining beneficiary in the following order: first to my wife Millicent, second to my daughter, Sarah, third to my daughter Camille, fourth to my brother Oswald and, God forbid, fifth to my Aunt Herman.

(BENEFICIARIES straighten up.)

WENDLE. To our maid of many years, Miss Ruby Pinkbottom, I leave as a small token of my appreciation for her stimulating domestic services, the pink satin sheets and the king-size water bed.

(RUBY squeals.)

WENDLE. To Wendle Weedle, my friend and personal confidant, for his tedious, trivial tidbits on trips to Tanzania and his laborious lectures in the library, I leave nothing. Nothing!

(CAMILLE sees CAMERON enter. She screams.)

CAMILLE. Aaah! Mr. Weedle ... Mr. Weedle. ... it's Cameron.

MUSIC CUE NO. 41

(*CAMERON staggers in. During the commotion, CAMILLE sits. HERMIONE positions herself USL. RUBY stands USR of CAMERON. OSWALD stands far USR. MILLICENT tends to a disheveled CAMERON—shirt untucked and unbuttoned, chest exposed, loose rope around wrists.*)

MILLICENT. (*Ad-libs her concern, then when all is settled ...*) You poor thing. Are you all right? Let me look at you. Thank God you're alive.
CAMERON. I'll be all right in a moment. Just give me a moment to breathe.
MILLICENT. Ruby, bring Cameron a chair.

(*RUBY obeys. CAMERON sits.*)

CAMERON. I need a cigarette.
MILLICENT. Bring him a cigarette.
RUBY. (*Offers a cigarette.*) Here, have one of mine. They're queen size.
CAMERON. (*Takes a cigarette.*) Thank you.
RUBY. Go ahead, take a drag.
WENDLE. Now, Mr. Worthleston, I assume you escaped from your kidnappers. Would you fill us in on the details of your escape?

CAMERON. (*Stands.*) Well, they blindfolded me, and they shoved me in the back of a van. Yeah, that's it ... a van. After driving me around for ten minutes, they stopped and made me make the phone call asking for ransom. We drove some more, then they stopped at a shopping mall. When they went in, I managed to loosen the rope around my hands ... and I escaped.

WENDLE. Where was this shopping mall?

CAMERON. Fifth Avenue.

WENDLE. Fifth Avenue?

CAMERON. Yeah, (*Singing.*) the avenue, Fifth Avenue.

WENDLE. Did you get the license plate number?

CAMERON. No, I just ran.

WENDLE. You just ran.

CAMERON. I just ran.

WENDLE. Mr. Worthleston, what did your kidnappers look like?

CAMERON. The one who gagged and blindfolded me (*Notices CHADWICK as CHADWICK drops his napkin, stands to retrieve it.*) was a tall man around 50-55 years old, and he had a pleasant voice.

(*CHADWICK clears throat.*)

CAMERON. I didn't see what he looked like. He abducted me from behind.

WENDLE. (*Walks behind CAMERON and mimes abduction from behind.*) If he took you from behind, how did you know he was tall?
CAMERON. He had to be to blindfold and gag me, didn't he?
OSWALD. (*Comes forward and taps CAMERON on the leg with cane.*) Were you ill-treated or physically abused in any way?
CAMERON. Not really.
OSWALD. Pity. Young people don't know how to have fun these days.
WENDLE. Oswald, please ...

(*OSWALD makes his way back to his seat with the help of BARONESS.*)

WENDLE. A few more questions, Mr. Worthleston. You and Sarah were engaged to be married, weren't you?
CAMERON. Yes.
WENDLE. When?
CAMERON. Well ...
WENDLE. You seem a little uncertain. Mr. Worthleston, I searched Sarah's bedroom after her murder, and I found this. (*Presents Sarah's wedding ring.*)

MUSIC CUE NO. 42

WENDLE. Can you explain it?
CAMERON. It's a ring. Hey, what is this? I could have been killed just now.

WENDLE. What kind of ring?
CAMERON. It's Sarah's wedding ring.

MUSIC CUE NO. 43

WENDLE. Oh ...
CAMERON. Well, you're going to find out sooner or later. Sarah and I were secretly married this morning.
MILLICENT. Chadwick, I'm going to faint.
WENDLE. Mr. Worthleston, please tell us why you married Sarah Rutherford in secrecy.
CAMERON. She thought it was more romantic that way—you know like Romeo and Juliet.
HERMIONE. (*Stands*.) Oh yes, and I'm Hamlet's Ophelia. "Now let's see that noble and most sovereign reason/...O, woe is me/T'have seen what I have seen, ..."

(*MILLICENT motions CHADWICK to seat HERMIONE.*)

CHADWICK. Come along, Ophelia. Let's go back to Elsinore.
HERMIONE. Yes, Hamlet is due back momentarily, and I must be composed.
CHADWICK. We'll have the nunnery pick you up in the morning. You can *de*compose there. (*He sits her*.) You may continue, Weedle.
WENDLE. Yes. So you secretly married Sarah because she thought it romantic.
CAMERON. Yes.

CAMILLE. (*Stands, loud.*) NO!

MUSIC CUE NO. 44

CAMILLE. You see, Mr. Weedle, there was a prenuptial agreement between Sarah and Cameron which entitled Cameron to 10% of Sarah's inheritance, be she alive or dead.
WENDLE. How did you know of such an agreement?
CAMILLE. Sarah told me about it.
WENDLE. Is this true, Mr. Worthleston?
CAMERON. Yes. And it's perfectly legal. As a matter of fact, it was Sarah's idea.
WENDLE. Millicent, did you know about this?
MILLICENT. I knew about the agreement. I did not know about the marriage.
WENDLE. That will be all for the moment, Mr. Worthleston. I'm going to contact the police and inform them of your amazing recovery. (*Starts to exit.*)

MUSIC CUE NO. 45

CAMERON. (*Presents rope from wrists.*) Um ... I believe this is evidence or something.
WENDLE. (*Takes rope.*) Something. (*Exits.*)
CAMERON. Is there any food left?

(*RUBY presents an apple.*)

RUBY. Here you are, Cameron.

CAMERON. Thank you. You're very nice.

(*CAMERON grabs for the apple. RUBY lifts it out of reach.*)

RUBY. You want nice? Meet me in the west wing, I'll show you nice. (*Squeals.*) Go ahead and open the second and only the second seal on your dossiers folks. I gotta go prepare for my twilight rendezvous. Maestro, how about something romantic?

MUSIC CUE NO. 46
(*Popular romantic standard.*)

RUBY. (*Replaces Cameron's chair with dramatic movement.*) Be still my aching heart. (*Poses then exits.*)

(*CAMERON and all others work tables. Dessert and coffee are served.*
Guests open next clue—a telegram which reads:
Date: August 29, (*Year is fifteen years ago.*)
From:
Lipschitz, Lipschitz and Lipschitz
Attorneys at Law
Central Tower
703 Market Street
San Francisco, CA 94103

To:
Rutherford Tea and Spice Imports

690 Market Street
San Francisco, CA 94104
Attn: Mssrs. Oswald and William Rutherford

Gentlemen:
Please be advised that yesterday Thomas, Calahan, President of Pacific Tea Company terminated bankruptcy proceedings and finally agreed to transfer all 200 shares of Pacific Tea to Rutherford Tea and Spice Imports. Sale price was on our terms.)

Scene 5

9:20 p.m./2:35 p.m.

(When cued, MILLICENT stands front and center and rings bell and calls for RUBY, who is off to the side.
MUSIC: Out.)

MILLICENT. Ruby. Oh Ruby.

(RUBY approaches MILLICENT.)

MILLICENT. Ruby, I'd like a brief, quiet word with you. (*Now exaggerated and loud.*) *Who* is responsible for hiring the wait staff?

MUSIC CUE NO. 47

(*MILLICENT walks away. RUBY follows.*)

RUBY. Why I am, Ma'am. You know that.
MILLICENT. And Ruby, who is responsible for the pacing of the dinner?

MUSIC CUE NO. 48 (*Same as above.*)

RUBY. I am, Ma'am.
MILLICENT. And who is responsible for keeping Hermione where she belongs—away from the guests?

MUSIC CUE NO. 49 (*Same as above.*)

RUBY. Well, Ma'am, I wanted to talk to you about that. You see ...
MILLICENT. (*Angry.*) I am not finished, Ruby. Dinner has been behind schedule all evening. And what perturbs me most is that Oswald informs me you didn't have the red wine uncorked 20 minutes before serving it, so that it could breathe.
RUBY. What right does Oswald have giving progress reports on me? I have been a devoted, conscientious employee for fifteen year. You've never liked him. You've never trusted him. Why now, Millicent? Huh? Why now? (*Beat.*) Oswald, I'd like a word with you.

MUSIC CUE NO. 50

(RUBY storms over to OSWALD, and slaps him on either cheek.)

MUSIC CUE NO. 51

(RUBY dramatically exits.)

OSWALD. Ruby, you're getting more like Millicent everyday. You're putting too much NutraSweet on your prunes. (*Beat.*) Baroness, how about cheering me up with another round of...
BARONESS & OSWALD. Sink the Bismark!

(They laugh.)

CAMERON. (*Stands.*) Uh, Tr ... Baroness, when you're done maybe I can get some basic training.
BARONESS. Anything for you, sweetheart.
CAMILLE. (*Stands.*) You know, I can't believe your behavior. All of you. Uncle Oswald, I don't think it's fair to make light of Ruby's emotion—she's upset. And Cameron, I'm so surprised at you! Your fiancee .. your wife was just murdered, yet you continue to joke around and (*Refers to open shirt.*) display your ignorance.

CAMERON. (*Closes his shirt.*) Hey look, no Alice in Wonderland is going to tell me what I should think.

CAMILLE. Do you think, Cameron? Do you? I wonder.

CAMERON. Listen, Camille, where were you when Sarah was shot?

CAMILLE. How dare you imply that I would kill my own sister. Sarah was probably the only person in this house except Uncle Oswald who understood me, who listened to me. Kill her? Kill Sarah? Oh, Cameron you are pathetic. (*She slaps him. HERMIONE claps.*)

MUSIC CUE NO. 52

(*CAMILLE storms out.*)

CAMERON. I get no respect. Oh well, I guess I'll go get cleaned up.

BARONESS. Don't forget to keep your shirt open when you come back.

(*CAMERON exits.*)

BARONESS. I think it's time to entertain the troops. (*Walks forward.*) You know I was the pin-up girl for the Luftwafer. (*Poses.*) We all knew dear Wilhelm, (*Sneers at Millicent.*) some of us more intimately than others. I remember the night I heard of Wilhelm's death. I was visiting my mother and my brother in Modesto ...

WENDLE. Modesto, West Germany?
BARONESS. No. Modesto, California—where Gallo wine is made. I sing this song for Wilhelm. It's like Deutschland and America coming together. Schatzi.

MUSIC CUE NO. 53

(*BARONESS sings an upbeat country-western sytle song,in the middle of which she yodels. She ends the song miming the shooting of two pistols one in each hand.*)

MILLICENT. I'm not going to stay while this trollop sings in my house. I'm leaving. (*Beckoning him.*) Chadwick!
CHADWICK. (*Mimicking the Baroness' last pose.*) Bang, bang.

(*MILLICENT and CHADWICK exit.*)

BARONESS. Now that the schtick in the mud is gone. Let's party. I remember visiting Paris with Wilhelm. We would sit on the banks of the Seine and sip Wilhelm's favorite liquer "Peaches and Cream"—he would call me Peaches, I would call him Cream. Wilhelm, of course, is no longer here ... Ozzie, Ozzie, you come up here. I sing to you.

(*OSWALD, like a child, runs to BARONESS.*)

BARONESS. Is everybody ready? Schatzi.

MUSIC CUE NO. 54

(*BARONESS sings a popular German song à la Dietrich. At the end of the second "A," two gunshots ring out. OSWALD staggers comedically, then falls to the floor. WENDLE runs to OSWALD to check for breathing. MILLICENT, CHADWICK, CAMILLE and CAMERON reenter.*)

WENDLE. Please, quiet everyone. He's breathing. He's trying to say something.
BARONESS. Who cares about his breathing! What about my hand—I'll never sing again.

(*A waiter enters with a bandage for BARONESS' hand.*)

WENDLE. He's saying something.
OSWALD. Beware the guise. (*He dies.*)
WENDLE. He's dead.
MILLICENT. What did he say?
WENDLE. He said ...

MUSIC CUE NO. 55

OSWALD. (*Sits up.*) Beware the guise.
BARONESS. Which guys—you guys?

MILLICENT. Oh, get him out of here.

MUSIC CUE NO. 56 (*Funeral march.*)

(*OSWALD is carried out on a stretcher. MILLICENT, CHADWICK, CAMERON and CAMILLE sit.*)

WENDLE. Ladies and gentlemen, this senseless killing must stop. I will now be conducting my "Parade of Suspects." In this interrogation you will have the opportunity to question the suspects, when I have finished with them. (*Beat.*) Now, after searching the entire house, I found a blue terry cloth robe in Millicent's bedroom with the monogram C.W. on it. Also, downstairs in the coatroom I found a Burberry raincoat, in the pocket of this raincoat, I found this note. Mr. Worthleston, please stand. I ask you to stand, because the monogram and the raincoat are yours.

(*CAMERON stands.*)

WENDLE. Who is Trixie?
CAMERON. I don't know.
WENDLE. Maybe if I read the note, it will refresh your memory. "Dear Cam, I await our twilight rendezvous, Lover. We must complete our scheme before then." And it's signed Trixie C.

CAMERON. I've never seen that note before. Someone must have put it in my coat, trying to implicate me in all that has happened.

CHADWICK. Well, I'd like to know what your bath robe was doing in my Millicent's bedroom. Millicent?

MUSIC CUE NO. 57

MILLICENT. I'll explain ... later.

WENDLE. Mr. Worthleston, have you ever lived on the west coast?

CAMERON. Not since The Beverly Hillbillies left.

WENDLE. So you left at an early age.

CAMERON. No, I was young.

WENDLE. What does your family do for a living?

CAMERON. My mother sells Mary Kay cosmetics. My father was a nobleman of sorts. The bum left us when I was young.

WENDLE. Were you faithful to Sarah?

CAMERON. Yeah ... mostly.

WENDLE. How much do you stand to inherit from the prenuptial agreement?

CAMERON. I don't know. Around 6 million, 743 thousand and 264 dollars.

WENDLE. Are there any questions for Mr. Worthleston?

(WENDLE entertains questions from the guests. After questioning, CAMERON sits.)

WENDLE. Next, Millicent. Would you please stand? (*She stands.*) For as long as I have known you, I have never known your maiden name.

MILLICENT. It was ... Bogwater.

WENDLE. We're all aware that the Rutherford family business is tea and spice importing, what did your family do?

MILLICENT. They were in fish.

BARONESS. Und chips.

WENDLE. William left all of the shares of Rutherford Tea and Spice to his brother Oswald. Now that Oswald is dead, these shares become yours. Where were you when Oswald was shot?

MILLICENT. In the loo.

WENDLE. Did anyone see you there?

MILLICENT. I certainly hope not.

WENDLE. Now that Sarah is dead, you own an additional 30% of the estate. It pains me to ask this, but did you kill your daughter?

MILLICENT. Of course not.

WENDLE. (*Fast.*) Ever been named Trixie?

MILLICENT. Never.

WENDLE. Are there any questions for Millicent Rutherford?

(*WENDLE entertains questions from the guests. After questioning, MILLICENT sits.*)

WENDLE. Mr. Chadwick Sterling, would you please stand? (*He stands.*) How long have you known Millicent?

CHADWICK. Eight glorious months.
WENDLE. How did you meet?
CHADWICK. We met a mutual friend's film opening in Los Angeles.
WENDLE. You're quite a traveler, Mr. Sterling.
CHADWICK. It comes with the territory. I own textile factories here and there.
WENDLE. Have you ever lived on the west coast?
CHADWICK. No.
WENDLE. Owned any other industries?
CHADWICK. Back in the seventies, I owned a chain of Wee Willy Winky Motels, and I bought and sold tea for a while.
WENDLE. Tea. Where?
CHADWICK. In the south: Georgia, Alabama, Louisiana.
WENDLE. What were you doing in London?
CHADWICK. I was meeting with a man who was interested in opening an English factory.
WENDLE. And why did you return early?
CHADWICK. I ... I found out that my business has collapsed, and I was bankrupt.
MILLICENT. Chadwick, why didn't you tell me?
CHADWICK. With all that was going on, it wasn't the right time.
MILLICENT. How can you underestimate the importance of this?
CHADWICK. Now is not the time to discuss the matter.

MILLICENT. Oh yes it is, Chadwick!

CHADWICK. (*Angry.*) So, Millicent your true colors finally surface. Money and macho libertines—that's all you're interested in, isn't it? Your capacity to love and to give is governed solely by the monetary value of our relationship. That's it.

MILLICENT. Chadwick, you're wounding me.

WENDLE. All right you two, enough. Are there any questions for Mr. Sterling? (*Entertains questions.*) Thank you, Mr. Sterling. (*He sits.*) Now, Ruby Pinkbottom. Won't you tell us why Lord Rutherford left you the pink satin sheets and the water bed?

RUBY. You see, one day I was makin' up the sheets on the water bed and Lord Rutherford sneaks up behind me and pinches me on the bum. Yes he did. So I said, "Lord Rutherford you look here." And he looked there. After that I straightened him out, so to speak.

(*WENDLE entertains questions for RUBY. Optional: He questions a garrulous guest who is very involved.*)

WENDLE. Baroness, please stand. (*She stands.*) Baroness, you are a well-traveled and I'm sure a very experienced woman. Are you involved with any of the men in this room?

BARONESS. (*Snaps her head left, then slowly pans the room.*) Well, Oswald, who is no longer in the room, and I did a little noshing in the closet earlier.

WENDLE. Yes, we all remember when Oswald came out of the closet. Baroness, had you ever met Oswald before tonight?

BARONESS. I don't think so.

WENDLE. What does that mean?

BARONESS. Well, if you met one Rutherford, you've met them all.

WENDLE. How about Chadwick Sterling? Any twilight rendezvous with him?

BARONESS. (*A la Mae West.*) If he's asking, I'm acceptin'.

WENDLE. How about Cameron?

BARONESS. (*Abrupt.*) Listen, I don't see why my personal life is always the topic of conversation. After all, I haven't had as much experience as the lady of the house.

MILLICENT. That's enough. Baroness, you keep your filthy mouth off me and my family and my guests.

BARONESS. Your family and your guests. Ha! They are not your family, and they are not your guests. And why would I want to touch any of them? You've had them all already.

MILLICENT. Well, I never.

BARONESS. Oh, yes you did. Und I vill prove it, right here and now. Meine Dammen und Herren, we are going to play a little game called "To Tell the Truth." Now Lady Rutherford claims that she is respectable widow ... black widow maybe. I want to know who in this room has slept with or done the nasties with Millicent Rutherford? (*Strong.*) Stand up now!

MUSIC CUE NO. 59

(*Per their character assignments, guests know if they have been involved with MILLICENT. All male guests and several female guests stand.*)

BARONESS. Ha! What did I tell you?

MUSIC CUE NO. 60

BARONESS. That's why the lady is a tramp. Case closed.
MILLICENT. Wait, wait, wait. (*She runs up to one man.*) This *one* is not telling the truth.

MUSIC CUE NO. 61A

(*Next bit done with melodramatic finesse a la "Dark Victory."*)

CHADWICK. (*Rises.*) Millicent.
MILLICENT. Chadwick.
CHADWICK. Millicent, is this true?
MILLICENT. Oh, Chadwick.
CHADWICK. Oh, Millicent.
MILLICENT. Chadwick, I was lonely after William's death. A girl needs companionship in her hour of need. (*Harsh cockney.*) Oh, Chadwick you must understand.

CHADWICK. I *am* understanding. (*Aside.*) But this is a bit much.

MILLICENT. I was wrong Chadwick. I love you. Do please forgive me.

CHADWICK. Of course I forgive you.

MILLICENT. (*Aside.*) Why?

MUSIC CUE NO. 61B

CHADWICK. I'll explain ... later. (*CHADWICK dips MILLICENT and kisses her.*) [MUSIC CUE NO. 61C]

BARONESS. I think I'm gonna be sick.

WENDLE. Ladies and gentlemen, I now know who the killer is. I'll need a few moments to organize my facts. And then I will be prepared to make at least one arrest. At this time you can offer your own solution to these crimes. Please open the final seal on your dossier. You will find your resolution form. Please fill it in expeditiously. They will be collected shortly. Justice will prevail. Truth will come to light. Good luck. (*Exits.*)

MUSIC CUE NO. 62
(Variations on MRH Theme. Segue to classical background.)

Scene 6
The Resolution
9:50 p.m./3:05 p.m.

(*WENDLE enters. MUSIC: Out.*)

WENDLE. Ladies and gentlemen, after much deliberation, I now know who the killer is

MUSIC CUE NO. 63

WENDLE. Or should I say, killers are. Yes, because two people, one duet was responsible for offing Sarah and Oswald Rutherford—two unfortunate members of the same amoral clan.
MILLICENT. I object to that remark!
WENDLE. Overruled! Ladies and gentlemen, as Balzac said, "Behind every fortune there is a crime." Behind the Rutherford fortune there is murder. The two killers were a man and a woman. Who was this duo, and what did they want? Let's look at some of the evidence. We have a limerick that tells us of an "unlikely duet who lives a secret well-kept. Each has a call to perpetrate one fall. Deceit is an art at which both are adept." Yes, each had a call. One killed for greed. The other, the mastermind of this plot, for revenge. The writing was on the wall, or should I say the mirror. (*Motioning across large mirror.*) "I've waited 15 years for this." Years for revenge. Revenge for what? First let's find our duet. Camille ...

MUSIC CUE NO. 64

CAMILLE. You couldn't mean me.

WENDLE. You're all alone tonight—an attractive charming, young lady, unescorted.

CAMILLE. What are you talking about?

WENDLE. Well, it seems so unusual that you should be alone tonight. Or are you alone?

CAMILLE. Yes. I mean no. I mean my family is here with me.

WENDLE. *Your* family. You mean the family that made you a black sheep since your father was no longer around to take care of you?

CAMILLE. Uncle Oswald takes ... Uncle Oswald took care of me.

WENDLE. Yes, Uncle Oswald. You two made an interesting duo. His greed and your desire to get back at the family who shunned you might have motivated a little killing tonight.

CAMILLE. No.

WENDLE. Many of you saw the gun fall out of Oswald's bag when he arrived tonight. After Sarah was out of the way, your call had been answered. Did you kill your Uncle Oswald?

CAMILLE. I didn't kill Uncle Oswald. I loved Uncle Oswald. I couldn't kill Uncle Oswald.

MILLICENT. Of course she could.

WENDLE. No. Millicent. She couldn't. Oswald was the only one who treated her decently. If she wanted to kill, she might have shot you. No, ladies and gentlemen, it wasn't

Camille. But there's another black sheep of sorts who may have had motive: Ruby Pinkbottom ...

MUSIC CUE NO. 65

WENDLE. Loyal maid to the Rutherford family for *so* many years.
RUBY. Weedle, I find your accusations unfounded and appalling.
WENDLE. It seems that someone who is servile to the demanding Millicent Rutherford might have expected a little more in the will
RUBY. I did. I did. But I didn't kill anyone.
WENDLE. Ruby, I believe you. However, you possess certain information which was essential to my solving of this case. Won't you share that information with us?
MILLICENT. Ruby don't say a word. If Wendle is so sure that one of us or two of us are killers, let him prove it.
WENDLE. Millicent, your turn will come. But first, Ruby, what can you tell us about the Rutherford Tea and Spice Company taking over a competing concern called Pacific Tea.
RUBY. I remember it well. It was _____ (*Insert date fifteen years ago.*). Oswald and William were trying to monopolize the tea business in the United States. They strong-armed Pacific Tea, forced them into bankruptcy, then bought them out for a ridiculously low price.
MILLICENT. Ruby, you're sacked.

RUBY. Sacked? Oh well, what's one more pink slip.

MUSIC CUE NO. 66

(RUBY tosses duster and exits.)

WENDLE. Ladies and gentlemen, who masterminded the plot and who killed for greed? Chadwick Sterling ...

MUSIC CUE NO. 67

WENDLE. Please stand.
MILLICENT. You leave him out of this.
CHADWICK. *(Rises.)* Yes, what is it?
WENDLE. You're an entrepreneur, a man of many travels and many businesses. You and Millicent make an interesting couple. She's certainly greedy and ...
CHADWICK. You leave her out of this Millicent is innocent.
WENDLE. Mr. Sterling, you've done business in the tea import industry. Could your company be the one William and Oswald Rutherford forced into bankruptcy? Are you here avenging them?
CHADWICK. No. Absolutely not.
WENDLE. You arrived after the first murder, and you were out of the room during the second.
CHADWICK. Purely circumstantial evidence.
WENDLE. What about your tea company?

CHADWICK. I did business in the south, not on the west coast.

MILLICENT. He knows nothing of Pacific Tea.

WENDLE. Well, if it's not Chadwick, there's another we can pair you with.

MILLICENT. Take care, Wendle. You're not in my league.

WENDLE. Let's stay on the subject of murder and revenge. Millicent, you're after all you can get?

MILLICENT. Right. But I don't kill for it.

WENDLE. You could have masterminded the plan and brought someone to do the killing for you.

MILLICENT. Who?

WENDLE. (*Pause.*) Cameron.

MUSIC CUE NO. 68

CAMERON. What's this guy saying? He doesn't know what he's talking about.

MILLICENT. Cameron is ...

CAMERON. Cameron is what?

MILLICENT. Cameron was just a fling, a casual affair. You were away . I was lonely. He was a poor substitute, nothing more.

WENDLE. But you trusted him, Millicent. Perhaps you trusted him too much. The note from Trixie C.: "I await our twilight rendezvous, *Lover.*" Couldn't you see he was using you and your daughter Sarah?

MILLICENT. No. I couldn't.

CAMERON. He's lying, Millicent. He's lying.

WENDLE. Mr. Worthleston, you are money hungry and you stop at nothing to get it.

CAMERON. You're lying!

WENDLE. You conned Millicent, you staged your own kidnapping, you killed Sarah and Oswald Rutherford, and you did it all for money!

CAMERON. No. No. I didn't.

WENDLE. (*Strong.*) Yes. Yes. You did. And you weren't alone. Your revengeful lover masterminded the plan, and you executed it.

CAMERON. (*To the Baroness, breaking down.*) I told you we had enough. We should have stopped. I told you!

BARONESS. (*Standing.*) You fool. Shut up. It's all circumstantial evidence.

MUSIC CUE NO. 69

WENDLE. Circumstantial? (*Points at BARONESS.*) Trixie C. is Trixie Calahan, daughter of Thomas Calahan, President of Pacific Tea Company, who came here tonight to make the entire Rutherford family pay for the destruction it caused her father's business 15 years ago.

BARONESS. You're crazy. You have nothing.

MUSIC CUE NO. 70

WENDLE. (*Dangling the Pacific Tea bag.*) I have the Pacific tea bag from your cup.

MUSIC CUE NO. 71

BARONESS. Yes. (*Pulls off wig, drops German accent, now sounds gruff.*) Yes, we did it. And I'm glad we did it. They ruined my Poppa, so I ruined them.

(*BARONESS pulls gun, as she starts to exit. CAMERON follows, grabbing a spoon off a table and pointing it at guests for protection.*)

BARONESS. (*Moving toward center.*) Watch out. This is a small gun, but it shoots big bullets. Cameron, get the Mercedes.

(*MILLICENT pulls a gun and shoots BARONESS.*)

BARONESS. Cameron, get the ambulance instead.

(*MILLICENT shoots CAMERON. He hits the wall and slides down.*)

BARONESS. Never mind.
WENDLE. There you have it, ladies and gentlemen, *Murder at Rutherford House*.

MUSIC CUE NO. 72A (*MRH Theme.*)

Bows.
Awards.

MUSIC CUES NO.'s 72B, 72C

End of Play

THE CLUES

1. **LIMERICK**
   There is an unlikely duet
   Who lives a secret well-kept
   Each has a call
   To perpetrate one fall
   Deceit is an art at which both are adept

   With heightened malevolence and greed
   A vow of destruction they would heed
   Their plot well-planned
   The duo would stand
   Against the clan of amoral creed

2. **TELEGRAM** - to be dated 15 years prior to performance date.
   From:
   Lipschitz, Lipschitz and Lipschitz
   Attorneys at Law
   Central Tower
   703 Market Street
   San Francisco, CA 94103

   To:
   Rutherford Tea and Spice Imports
   690 Market Street
   San Francisco, CA 94104
   Attn: Messrs. William and Oswald
     Rutherford

(contd.)

MURDER AT RUTHERFORD HOUSE 81

Gentlemen:
Please be advised that yesterday Thomas Calahan, President of Pacific Tea Company terminated bankruptcy proceedings and finally agreed to transfer all 200 shares of Pacific Tea to Rutherford Tea and Spice Imports. Sale price was on our terms.

3. BATHROOM MIRROR CLUE: I've waited 15 years for this.

4. CAMERON'S PRENUPTIAL AGREEMENT/SARAH'S WEDDING RING.

5. BARONESS' Pacific Co. tea bag.

6. HERMIONE's Rhyme (See script p.47.)

7. TRIXIE'S NOTE:
Dear Cam, I await our twilight rendezvous, Lover. We must complete our scheme before then. Trixie C.

8. BRIBE CLUES: (See script p. 42.)

9. OSWALD'S DYING MESSAGE: "Beware the guise."

PROPS

Black silk-like material (approx. 2 yds.)
Covered urn
Will rolled and tied with ribbon (in urn)
Shopping bag (OSWALD)
Items for OSWALD's bag: garish bra, prop gun, CAMILLE's gift-wrapped present.
3 starter pistols with blanks
2 additional prop pistols (HERMIONE/BARONESS)
Ear plugs
Cigarettes (RUBY)
Cigarette Lighter (RUBY)
Plastic apple (RUBY)
Butterfly net (WENDLE)
Sm. Silver tray (RUBY)
Bell (RUBY)
Feather Duster (RUBY)
White linen handkerchief embroidered with "CAM"
Cordless phone or one with a long cord
Rope (CAMERON)
Burnt cork (CAMERON)
Invitation (BARONESS)
Bloodied bandage (BARONESS)
Blind person's cane (OSWALD)
Sarah's wedding ring (WENDLE)
Sedative (RUBY)
Large spoon (RUBY)
Over-night bag (CHADWICK)
Lipstick (clue on mirror)

Rutherford tea centerpieces (1 per table)
Brewed cup of tea, on saucer a used Pacific tea bag with the label dangling (BARONESS)
Stretcher and white sheet

Paper Props and Supplies

Larry Looselipps letter
Cameron's ransom note
Love note from Trixie C.
2 award certificates
7 reserve signs for actors' seating at dining tables

Set Pieces

Table or pedestal for urn
2 chairs

Costume Pieces

Engagement ring (SARAH)
Blind, circular Sunglasses (OSWALD)

Suggested Performance/Meal Itinerary-Dinner

7:30 p.m.   DOORS OPEN
                 —Guests receive dossiers and character assignments

7:45 p.m.	SCENE 1 –Characters' entrances –Murder #1 (Sarah)
7:55 p.m.	COURSE #1 SERVED (at end of Scene 1, when cued)
8:05 p.m.	SCENE 2 –Baroness & Oswald in closet –Hermione shoots pigeons –Guests receive limerick clue
8:15 P.M.	COURSE #1 CLEARED
8:20 p.m.	COURSE #2 (when cued)
8:25 p.m.	SCENES 3 and 4 –Report on Murder #1 –Chadwick's entrance –Cameron kidnapping call –Guests bribe characters
8:35 p.m.	COURSE #2 CLEARED
8:40 p.m.	MAIN COURSE SERVED (when cued)

8:50 p.m.	SCENE 5 —Oswald's toast —Reading of will —Cameron returns —Guests receive telegram clue
9:10 p.m.	MAIN COURSE CLEARED
9:15 p.m.	DESSERT AND COFFEE SERVED (no cue)
9:20 p.m.	SCENE 6 —Millicent scolds Ruby —Baroness sings —Murder #2 (Oswald) —Parade of Suspects
9:35 p.m.	GUESTS FILL OUT RESOLUTION FORMS COFFEE REFILLED
9:40 p.m.	RESOLUTION FORMS COLLECTED
9:50 p.m.	RESOLUTION
10:05 p.m.	BONUS AND REWARDS
10:15 p.m.	END

Suggested Performance/Meal Itinerary-Brunch

1:00 p.m.	DOORS OPEN —Guests receive dossiers and character assignments
1:05 p.m.	COMPLIMENTARY CHAMPAGNE - WINE SERVED
1:15 p.m.	SCENE 1 —Characters' entrances —Murder #1 (Sarah) SCENE 2 —Baroness & Oswald in closet —Hermione shoots pigeons —Guests receive limerick clue
1:30 p.m.	COURSE #1 (when cued at the end of Scene 2)
1:35 p.m.	SCENES 3 and 4 —Report on Murder #1 —Chadwick's entrance —Cameron kidnapping call —Guests bribe characters

1:45 p.m.	COURSE #1 CLEARED
1:55 p.m.	MAIN COURSE SERVED (when cued)
2:05 p.m.	SCENE 5 –Oswald's toast –Reading of will –Cameron returns –Guests receive telegram clue
2:25 p.m.	MAIN COURSE CLEARED
2:30 p.m.	DESSERT AND COFFEE SERVED (no cue)
2:35 p.m.	SCENE 6 –Millicent scolds Ruby –Baroness sings –Murder #2 (Oswald) –Parade of Suspects
2:50 p.m.	GUESTS FILL OUT RESOLUTION FORMS COFFEE REFILLED
2:55 p.m.	RESOLUTION FORMS COLLECTED
3:05 p.m.	RESOLUTION
3:20 p.m.	BONUS AND REWARDS
3:30 p.m.	END

NOTE TO PRODUCER

The "Murder at Rutherford House Production Guide" is available for a fee through Samuel French, Inc. The Guide includes the guest mystery dossier and character biographies that each guest can play throughout the performance.

The Guide includes character biography cards (92 males and 92 females) with names and bios that relate each of them to the Rutherford family. Each bio can be printed on small blue (for men) and small pink (for women) business cards that can be handed out to guests upon arrival at the theatre. Two samples are below. If you have more than 184 guests in your audience then either repeat character bios or create more of them.

Samples:

LARRY LOOSELIPS, Gigolo

You've slept with Millicent, but are presently and secretly involved with Sarah. You wrote a note threatening her to break off her engagement to Cameron.

ENNY PRICE, Socialite

A six-time divorcee, you are very wealthy and very bored. You're forever hiring gigolos. You get the best because you'll pay "any price." Cameron knows this. Beware of your ex-husband, Sayle Price. He knows this, too.

Also in the Production Guide is a sample three fold dossier on 8 1/2 x 14 paper that can be copied, folded, and sealed as indicated for each guest to use throughout the night with a small pencil. The dossier includes:

1) The rules of the game.
2) A blank clue card for jotting notes
3) The limerick
4) The bribe segment
5) The telegram
6) A resolution form

Note: The "Murder at Rutherford House Production Guide" does not replace the "Murder a La Carte Production Manual" which is suggested for all first-time producers of Murder a La Carte events.

www.ingramcontent.com/pod-product-compliance
Ingram Content Group UK Ltd.
Pitfield, Milton Keynes, MK11 3LW, UK
UKHW021825010725
460272UK00005B/32

9 780573 691959